Excellence

anti establishmentarianism

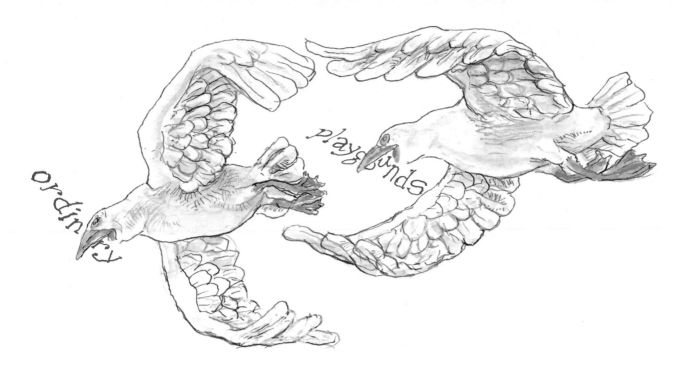

The WORD PIRATES

Susan Cooper
Steven Kellogg

NEAL PORTER BOOKS
HOLIDAY HOUSE / NEW YORK

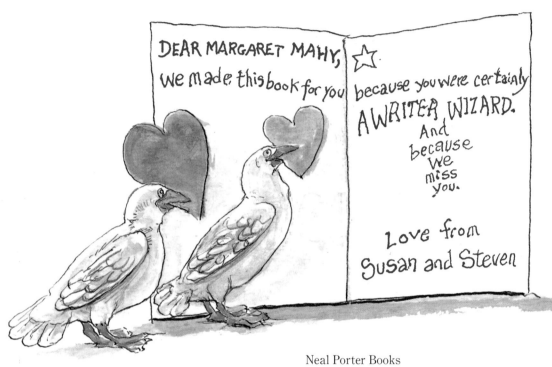

DEAR MARGARET MAHY,
We made this book for you ☆ because you were certainly
A WRITER WIZARD.
And because we miss you.

Love from
Susan and Steven

Neal Porter Books

Text copyright © 2019 by Susan Cooper
Illustrations copyright © 2019 by Steven Kellogg
All Rights Reserved
HOLIDAY HOUSE is registered in the U.S. Patent and Trademark Office.
Printed and bound in May 2019 by Toppan Leefung, DongGuan City, China.
The artwork for this book was created with a variety of materials including colored inks,
watercolors, colored pencils, and acrylic paints.
Book design by Jennifer Browne
www.holidayhouse.com
First Edition
1   3   5   7   9   10   8   6   4   2

Library of Congress Cataloging-in-Publication Data

Names: Cooper, Susan, 1935– author. | Kellogg, Steven, illustrator.
Title: The word pirates / by Susan Cooper ; pictures by Steven Kellogg.
Description: First edition. | New York : Holiday House, [2019] | "Neal Porter
Books." | Summary: When word-eating Captain Rottingbones and his crew
steal from the Word Wizard while she is telling a story, her pen proves
mightier than the pirates' swords.
Identifiers: LCCN 2018044040 | ISBN 9780823443598 (hardcover)
Subjects: | CYAC: Pirates—Fiction. | Wizards—Fiction. |
Storytelling—Fiction. | Vocabulary—Fiction.
Classification: LCC PZ7.C7878 Wor 2019 | DDC [E]—dc23 LC record available
at https://lccn.loc.gov/2018044040

It was early morning on the pirate ship.

"WORDS!"

roared Captain Rottingbones.

"Bring me fresh words! I need breakfast!"

Because that was what these pirates
ate, for breakfast, lunch and dinner.

WORDS.

"Aye aye, Captain!" shouted Fiddleface, the bosun.

So he let loose their flock of Bumblebirds.

They were trained to fly over the ocean and steal words fresh off the page, the minute that writers wrote them down.

Captain Rottingbones ate long chewy words, like
antidisestablishmentarianism. His crew liked short
crunchy words like *hop*, *fib*, *tuck*, *pop* and *zip*.
With milk.

And the Bumblebirds snapped up the broken bits
that fell on the deck.

All round the world the pirates sailed,
gobbling up words in every language.

Storytellers were heartbroken as the birds
peeled words off their pages,

ruining tales that would now never be heard or read!

But one day Captain Rottingbones grew greedy. He had learned of a Word Wizard, a zany New Zealander, whose stories were said to be so wonderful that he knew her words would be extra delicious.

He licked his lips.

"Yo ho, me hearties!" he cried. "Brush up the Bumblebirds!
We're sailing south!"

The Word Wizard lived on a green headland,
with her cats and her bouncy poodle, Baxter.

She was reading her magical stories to children, wearing her rainbow wig, when the birds swooped down.

Suddenly there were gaps in her story. It should have begun:
"Robert looked over his shoulder and there was a hippopotamus
following him." But now it said: "Robert . . . was a hippopotamus."

Her story was in tatters!

The Wizard was furious. So were the children. They ran after the birds as they flew to meet the pirates on the beach.

"GIVE US BACK OUR WORDS!" the children yelled.

"Your words are our lunch!" the pirates mumbled,
with their mouths full.

And they gobbled up every last one.

"Words were not made for you to eat!" the Wizard cried. "Words are for stories and poems, for friends, for singing and for dreams! Words are precious things!"

"We're pirates!" shouted Fiddleface. "We *steal* precious things! And we're hungry!"

Captain Rottingbones drew his sword.

"I'll fight you!" he snarled. "And when I win,
we'll eat every word you write!"

"Never!" thundered the Wizard. "Just you watch! A word-spinning pen is mightier than a pilfering pirate's sword!"

The captain leaped forward, his arm high.

But the Wizard raised her pen.

And out of the pen came all the magic of story.

The children shouted, "THE WORDS WIN!"

The End

The pirates were stunned. Their heads were buzzing
with stories. What amazing things words could do if you
didn't eat them! They stared at the Wizard, astonished.

The Wizard led them onto their ship, and with help from the children and the Bumblebirds, she sailed it to a faraway island.

She put the pirates ashore with
a big chest full of surprises.

"From this moment on," she said, "you are no longer Pilfering Pirates, you can be Fantabulous Farmers, and anything else you choose! Just remember always—words are food for imaginations, not for bellies!"

Then the Word Wizard sailed over the seven seas with her friends, spreading the news that the pirates had been defeated.

The storytellers were very much relieved, and
ever afterwards the words were safe in books.

Like this one.

While the pirates on their island learned, slowly, how to read—

and ate vegetables.

And one day the youngest pirate picked up a pen,

and, very carefully, began to write . . .